Dear Parent:
Your child's love of reading starts here!

Every child learns to read in a different way and at his or her own speed. Some go back and forth between reading levels and read favorite books again and again. Others read through each level in order. You can help your young reader improve and become more confident by encouraging his or her own interests and abilities. From books your child reads with you to the first books he or she reads alone, there are I Can Read Books for every stage of reading:

SHARED READING
Basic language, word repetition, and whimsical illustrations, ideal for sharing with your emergent reader

BEGINNING READING
Short sentences, familiar words, and simple concepts for children eager to read on their own

READING WITH HELP
Engaging stories, longer sentences, and language play for developing readers

READING ALONE
Complex plots, challenging vocabulary, and high-interest topics for the independent reader

ADVANCED READING
Short paragraphs, chapters, and exciting themes for the perfect bridge to chapter books

I Can Read Books have introduced children to the joy of reading since 1957. Featuring award-winning authors and illustrators and a fabulous cast of beloved characters, I Can Read Books set the standard for beginning readers.

A lifetime of discovery begins with the magical words "I Can Read!"

Visit www.icanread.com for information
on enriching your child's reading experience.

For Rebecca and Amanda Freedman,
two special young friends,
with love
—P.P.

For Elynor, my wife
—L.S.

HarperCollins®, 🐾®, and I Can Read Book® are trademarks of HarperCollins Publishers Inc.

Library of Congress Cataloging-in-Publication Data

Parish, Peggy.
    Amelia Bedelia helps out / Peggy Parish ; pictures by Lynn Sweat.
        p. cm.—(An I can read book)
    "Greenwillow Books"
    Summary: Amelia Bedelia shows her niece Effie Lou how to follow instructions to the letter as they dust the potato bugs and sew seeds.
    ISBN-10: 0-688-80231-1 (trade bdg.) — ISBN-13: 978-0-688-80231-8 (trade bdg.)
    ISBN-10: 0-688-84231-3 (lib. bdg.) — ISBN-13: 978-0-688-84231-4 (lib. bdg.)
    ISBN-10: 0-06-051111-7 (pbk.) — ISBN-13: 978-0-06-051111-1 (pbk.)
    [1. Amelia Bedelia (Fictitious character)—Juvenile fiction. 2. Humorous stories.] I. Sweat, Lynn, ill. II. Series.
PZ7.P219 Ap   79-11729
[E]   CIP
                                                                                                            AC

❖   Originally published by Greenwillow Books, an imprint of HarperCollins Publishers, in 1979.
10 11 12 13 SCP 20 19 18 17 16 15 14

Amelia Bedelia Helps Out

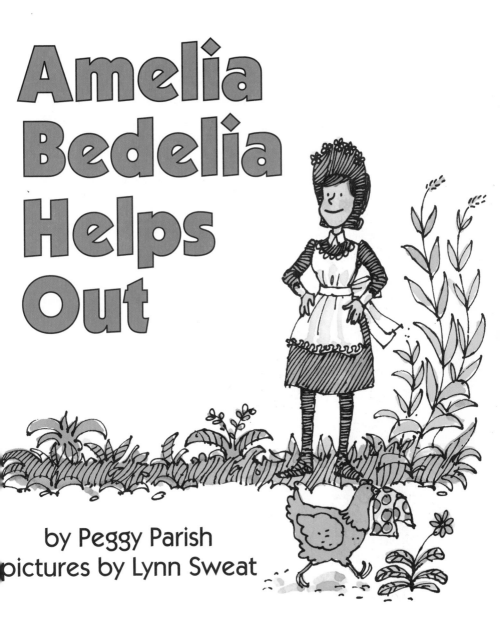

by Peggy Parish
pictures by Lynn Sweat

HarperCollins*Publishers*

"Have a good day,"

said Mr. Rogers.

"And you help your aunt,

Effie Lou."

"I will," said Effie Lou.

"I'll come back for you

late this afternoon,"

said Mr. Rogers.

He drove off.

"What a grand house," said Effie Lou.

"Miss Emma is a grand woman,"

said Amelia Bedelia.

She went to the door and knocked.

"Come in," called Miss Emma.
Amelia Bedelia and Effie Lou
went inside.

"I am glad to see you,"

said Miss Emma.

"Sumter is sick,

and my garden is a mess."

"Don't you fret," said Amelia Bedelia.

"We will take care of that.

Just tell us what to do."

"First," said Miss Emma,

"weed the garden."

"All right," said Amelia Bedelia.

"Is there anything else?"

"Yes," said Miss Emma.

"But go ahead

and start

before the sun gets hot."

9

"Come on, Effie Lou,"
said Amelia Bedelia.
"Let's get busy."
They went to the garden.
"It does have a lot of weeds,"
said Effie Lou.

She started to pull one.

"Stop!" said Amelia Bedelia.

"What are you doing?"

"Trying to get the weeds

out of the garden," said Effie Lou.

11

"Get them out!" said Amelia Bedelia.

"She said to weed the garden,

not unweed it."

"Oh," said Effie Lou. "I wonder

why she wants more weeds."

Amelia Bedelia thought.

"Those weeds are little," she said.

"Maybe vegetables get hot

just like people. They need

big weeds to shade them.

That's why Miss Emma told us

to weed before the sun gets hot."

"That makes sense," said Effie Lou.

"I see some really big weeds."

"Let's get them," said Amelia Bedelia.

They did.

Soon that garden was weeded.

Amelia Bedelia and Effie Lou

went back to the house.

"The garden is weeded,"

said Amelia Bedelia.

14

"Good," said Miss Emma.

"Now I want you to stake the beans.

Here is the string to tie them.

You can use this saw

to cut the stakes."

"All right," said Amelia Bedelia.

15

"There are bugs

on the potato plants.

Take this bug powder

and dust them,"

said Miss Emma.

"If you say so,"

said Amelia Bedelia.

The telephone rang.

Miss Emma went to answer it.

Amelia Bedelia found

all the things she needed.

She and Effie Lou

went back to the garden.

"All right," said Amelia Bedelia.

"We will steak the beans first."

"Have you ever done that?"

said Effie Lou.

"No," said Amelia Bedelia.

"But she just said to steak them.

Anybody can do that."

"Can I help?" said Effie Lou.

"Yes," said Amelia Bedelia.

"You count the bean plants."

Effie Lou counted and said,

"There are fifteen."

Amelia Bedelia

unwrapped a package.

She shook her head and said,

"That's a mighty little bit

of steak for fifteen plants.

But it was all she had."

She took the saw

and cut the steak

into fifteen pieces.

"I could have cut better

with a knife," Amelia Bedelia said.

"Why didn't you use one?"

said Effie Lou.

"Didn't Miss Emma say to use

this saw?" said Amelia Bedelia.

"Yes," said Effie Lou.

"Then that's why,"

said Amelia Bedelia.

"Now hold the steak while I tie it."

Amelia Bedelia and Effie Lou

steaked those beans.

"All right, beans,"

said Amelia Bedelia.

"Enjoy your steak."

Effie Lou laughed.

"Your work is fun," she said.

"That it is," said Amelia Bedelia.

"Now those bugs

are waiting to be dusted."

"How do we do that?"

said Effie Lou.

"I'll catch and you dust,"

said Amelia Bedelia.

"Here bug, here buggy, buggy, bug."

They caught and dusted every bug.

"Why did she want us to do that?"

said Effie Lou.

"Most people want bugs killed."

"But Miss Emma is not most people,"

said Amelia Bedelia.

"Those bugs may be her pets.

They are pretty little things."

"If you like bugs,"

said Effie Lou.

"That takes care of that,"

said Amelia Bedelia.

"Let's go in."

"I made lunch for you,"

called Miss Emma.

"After you eat,

throw some scraps

to the chickens."

"All right," said Amelia Bedelia.

"And Amelia Bedelia,"

said Miss Emma, "my garden club

is meeting here this afternoon.

Please make a tea cake."

"I'll be glad to," said Amelia Bedelia.

"I do love to bake."

Amelia Bedelia and Effie Lou
ate their lunch.
"I wonder where she keeps
her scraps?" said Amelia Bedelia.
"I'll ask her."

She went to Miss Emma's room.

She came right back.

"We will have to look for them,"

said Amelia Bedelia.

"She's asleep."

They looked and looked.

"Here's a whole bag of scraps,"

said Effie Lou.

"Good," said Amelia Bedelia.

"Take some and we'll throw them

to the chickens."

They went out to the chicken pen.

Effie Lou threw the scraps.

The chickens came running.

"Look at that!" said Amelia Bedelia.

"I never knew chickens

liked to play."

"Aren't they funny?" said Effie Lou.

"They sure are," said Amelia Bedelia.

"But I've got to get

that tea cake made."

"I never heard of tea cake,"
said Effie Lou.

"Neither have I," said Amelia Bedelia.

"Then how can you make one?"
said Effie Lou.

"Well," said Amelia Bedelia,
"I know what tea is, and I know
what cake is. I'll put them together
and I'll have tea cake."

"That's easy," said Effie Lou.

Amelia Bedelia got a mixing bowl.

She put a little of this

and some of that into it.

She mixed and she mixed.

"Now for the tea," she said.

Amelia Bedelia opened some tea bags

and mixed the tea into the batter.

"It looks awful," said Effie Lou.

"Different folks have different tastes,"

said Amelia Bedelia.

She poured the batter into a pan.

Soon that cake was baking.

Amelia Bedelia began to mix

another cake.

"What kind are you making now?"

said Effie Lou.

"Nut cake," said Amelia Bedelia.

"Miss Emma loves that."

Finally the cakes were baked.

"Are you going to put icing

on them?" said Effie Lou.

"That's a good idea,"

said Amelia Bedelia.

"It will fancy them up."

She mixed white icing

and pink icing.

"You ice the tea cake pink," she said.

"I'll ice the nut cake white."

They finished the cakes

and put them away.

Miss Emma came into the kitchen.

"The cake is ready,"

said Amelia Bedelia.

"It smells good," said Miss Emma.

"There's one more thing

I want you to do.

There is a bare spot in my front lawn.

Please sow these grass seeds on it."

"We will be glad to,"

said Amelia Bedelia.

"Come on, Effie Lou."

They went out front.

"That spot is bare," said Effie Lou.

"It sure is," said Amelia Bedelia.

She sat down and took two needles

and some thread from her bag.

She threaded the needles.

"Here is yours," she said.

"Now, let's sew."

Amelia Bedelia and Effie Lou

sewed those grass seeds

on the bare spot.

"Tie the ends together,"

said Amelia Bedelia.

"We don't want the seeds to fall off."

They went into the house.

Miss Emma was in the kitchen.

"Let's walk around some," she said.

"Show me what you've done."

"All right," said Amelia Bedelia.

They walked by the chicken pen.

"Land sakes!" said Miss Emma.

"What are those colored things?"

"Scraps," said Amelia Bedelia.

"Those chickens did have fun."

"My quilting pieces!" said Miss Emma.

"My good quilting pieces!"

"Did we use the wrong scraps?"

said Amelia Bedelia.

"Go get them, Effie Lou."

Miss Emma walked to the garden.

She stopped and stared.

"Those weeds!" she said.

"Those big weeds!"

"We got the biggest we could find,"

said Amelia Bedelia.

Miss Emma looked at Amelia Bedelia.

"Thank goodness Sumter

will be back soon," she said.

"Why didn't you stake the beans?"

"We did!" said Amelia Bedelia.

"There just wasn't much steak

to give them.

Show her, Effie Lou."

Effie Lou held up a bush.

"There goes my dinner,"

said Miss Emma.

She looked at the potatoes.

"I see the bugs are dead," she said.

"Dead!" said Amelia Bedelia.

"Did we dust them too much?

I'll get you some more."

Miss Emma laughed and said,

"I can live without them.

You've done enough."

"We enjoyed doing it,"

said Amelia Bedelia.

51

"I've seen all I want to see,"

said Miss Emma.

They all went inside.

"The ladies should be here soon,"

said Miss Emma.

"The table is set.

The tea is made.

You can put the cake on this tray."

"All right," said Amelia Bedelia.

"I'll let the ladies in,"

said Miss Emma.

She left the kitchen.

"Let's get the cakes ready,"

said Amelia Bedelia.

"I hear the ladies coming now."

53

Soon Miss Emma called,

"Amelia Bedelia,

please bring the tea."

"Coming," said Amelia Bedelia.

"Bring the cakes, Effie Lou."

Amelia Bedelia set the tea tray

in front of Miss Emma.

"Go ahead and pass the cake,"

said Miss Emma.

Every lady took some cake.

"I'm starved," said Mrs. Lee.

"I can't wait for the tea."

She bit into her cake.

"Delicious!" she said.

"I've never tasted this kind before."

"You've never tasted nut cake?"
said Miss Mary.

"This isn't nut cake," said Mrs. Lee.

"Try the pink kind."

"It is good,"

said Grandma Wilson.

"Hand me another piece."

"There," said Miss Emma,

"your tea is poured."

"Who cares about tea?"

said Mrs. Mark.

"I want more pink cake."

"Emma, do tell us what kind of cake this is," said Mrs. Bloom.

Miss Emma took some cake.

"My favorite," she said. "Nut cake."

"No, the pink kind," said Ella Jean.

"Try the pink kind."

But all the pink cake was gone.

"Stop keeping secrets,"

said Grandma Wilson.

"What kind of cake was that?"

"Ask Amelia Bedelia,"

said Miss Emma.

"She made it."

A car horn honked outside.

"Mr. Rogers!" said Amelia Bedelia.

"Come on, Effie Lou."

59

Miss Emma followed

Amelia Bedelia to the kitchen.

"What kind of cake was

the pink one?" she asked.

Amelia Bedelia looked puzzled.

"Tea cake," she said.

"That's what you said to make."

"Tea! You mean—" said Miss Emma.

She began to laugh.

Amelia Bedelia saw something.

"Oh, I plumb forgot," she said.

"Your grass seeds."

Miss Emma looked at them.

She laughed harder

and put them around her neck.

"Amelia Bedelia," she said,

"you are really something.

Effie Lou, you are lucky

to have Amelia Bedelia for an aunt."

"I know," said Effie Lou.

"Amelia Bedelia knows everything."

The horn honked again.

"Hurry, Effie Lou,"

said Amelia Bedelia.

"We can't keep Mr. Rogers waiting."

63